Oliver Button

is a

Sissy

OLIVER BUTTON

IS A

SISSY

Story and Pictures by

TOMIE dePAOLA

SIMON & SCHUSTER BOOKS FOR YOUNG READERS

New York   London   Toronto   Sydney   New Delhi

To Flossie

SIMON & SCHUSTER BOOKS FOR YOUNG READERS
An imprint of Simon & Schuster Children's Publishing Division
1230 Avenue of the Americas, New York, New York 10020
Copyright © 1979 by Tomie dePaola
All rights reserved, including the right of reproduction in whole or in part in any form.
SIMON & SCHUSTER BOOKS FOR YOUNG READERS is a trademark of Simon & Schuster,
Inc.
For information about special discounts for bulk purchases,
please contact Simon & Schuster Special Sales at 1-866-506-1949
or business@simonandschuster.com.
The Simon & Schuster Speakers Bureau can bring authors to your live event.
For more information or to book an event, contact the Simon & Schuster Speakers Bureau
at 1-866-248-3049 or visit our website at www.simonspeakers.com.
Book design by Laurent Linn
The text for this book was set in Brinar Pro.
Manufactured in China
0417 SCP
2 4 6 8 10 9 7 5 3 1
Library of Congress Cataloging-in-Publication Data
Names: DePaola, Tomie, 1934– author, illustrator.
Title: Oliver Button is a sissy / story and pictures by Tomie dePaola.
Description: First edition. | New York : Simon & Schuster Books for Young Readers, [2017], c1979. |
Summary: His classmates' taunts do not stop Oliver Button from doing what he likes best.
Identifiers: LCCN 2016028890 (print) | LCCN 2016057008 (eBook) | ISBN 9781481477574
(hardback) | ISBN 9781481477581 (eBook)
Subjects: | CYAC: Dance—Fiction. | Sex role—Fiction. | BISAC: JUVENILE FICTION / Performing Arts
/ Dance. | JUVENILE FICTION / Social Issues / Peer Pressure. | JUVENILE FICTION / Social Issues /
Self-Esteem & Self-Reliance.
Classification: LCC PZ7.D439 Ol 2017 (print) | LCC PZ7.D439 (eBook) | DDC [E]—dc23
LC record available at https://lccn.loc.gov/2016028890

Oliver Button was called a sissy.

He didn't like to do things that boys are supposed to do.

Instead, he liked to walk in the woods and play jump rope.

He liked to read books and draw pictures.

He even liked to play with paper dolls.

And Oliver Button liked to play dress-up.
He would go up to the attic and put on costumes.

Then he would sing and dance and make believe he was a movie star.

"Oliver," said his papa. "Don't be such a sissy! Go out
and play baseball or football or basketball. Any kind of ball!"

But Oliver didn't want to play any kind of ball. He didn't like to play ball because he wasn't very good at it. He dropped the ball or struck out or didn't run fast enough. And he was always the last person picked for any team.

"Oh, rats!" the captain would say. "We have to have Oliver Button. Now we'll lose for sure."

"Oliver," said Mama, "you have to play something. You
need your exercise."

"I get exercise, Mama," said Oliver. "I walk in the woods,
I play jump rope, and I love to dance.

"Watch!"

So Mama and Papa sent Oliver Button to
Ms. Leah's Dancing School.

"Especially for the exercise," Papa said.

Oliver Button got a nice, black, shiny pair of tap shoes.

And he practiced and practiced.

But the boys, especially the older ones, teased Oliver Button in the schoolyard.

"What are those shiny shoes, sissy?" they said.

"La-de-doo, you gonna dance for us?"

And they grabbed Oliver's tap shoes and played catch with them, until one of the girls caught them.

"You leave Oliver Button's tap shoes alone!" said the girls.
"Here, Oliver."

"Gotta have help from *girls*," the boys said teasingly.

And they wrote on the school wall:

Almost every day, the boys teased Oliver Button.

But Oliver Button kept on going to Ms. Leah's Dancing School every week, and he practiced and practiced.

One day a talent show was announced.

"Oliver," said Ms. Leah, "there's going to be a talent show at the movie theater on Sunday afternoon, one month from now. I would like you to be in it. I asked your mother and father, and they said it was up to you."

Oliver Button was all excited.

Ms. Leah helped him with his routine.

Mama made him a costume.

And Oliver practiced and practiced.

Finally it was the Friday before the big day.
"Class," the teacher said. "On Sunday afternoon
there will be a big talent show at the movie theater.

And one of your classmates is going to be in it.
I hope you will all go and cheer for Oliver Button."
"Sissy!" whispered the boys.

On Sunday afternoon, the movie theater was full.
One after the other, all the acts were performed.

There was a magician and an accordion player, a baton-twirler and a lady who sang about moon, June, and kissing.

Finally it was Oliver Button's turn. The piano player
started the music, and the spotlight came on.

Oliver Button stepped into it.

"Dum-de-dum," the music went. "Dum-de-dum-de-dum."
Oliver tapped and tapped.

"Dum-de-dum-de-dum-dum-DUM."
Oliver bowed and the audience clapped and clapped.

When all the acts were over, everybody came out on stage.

The master of ceremonies began to announce the prizes.

"And now, ladies and gentlemen, the winner of the first prize—
the little girl who did the baton-twirling, ROXIE VALENTINE!"
The audience cheered and whistled.

Oliver Button tried not to cry.

Mama, Papa, and Ms. Leah gave Oliver big hugs.

"Never mind," said Papa, "we are taking our great dancer out for a great pizza. I'm so proud of you."

"So are we!" said Mama and Ms. Leah.

Monday morning Oliver Button didn't want to go to school. "Now, now, Oliver," Mama said, "that's silly. Come on and eat your breakfast. You'll be late."

So Oliver went to school.

When the school bell rang, Oliver Button was the last to go in.

Then he noticed the school wall.

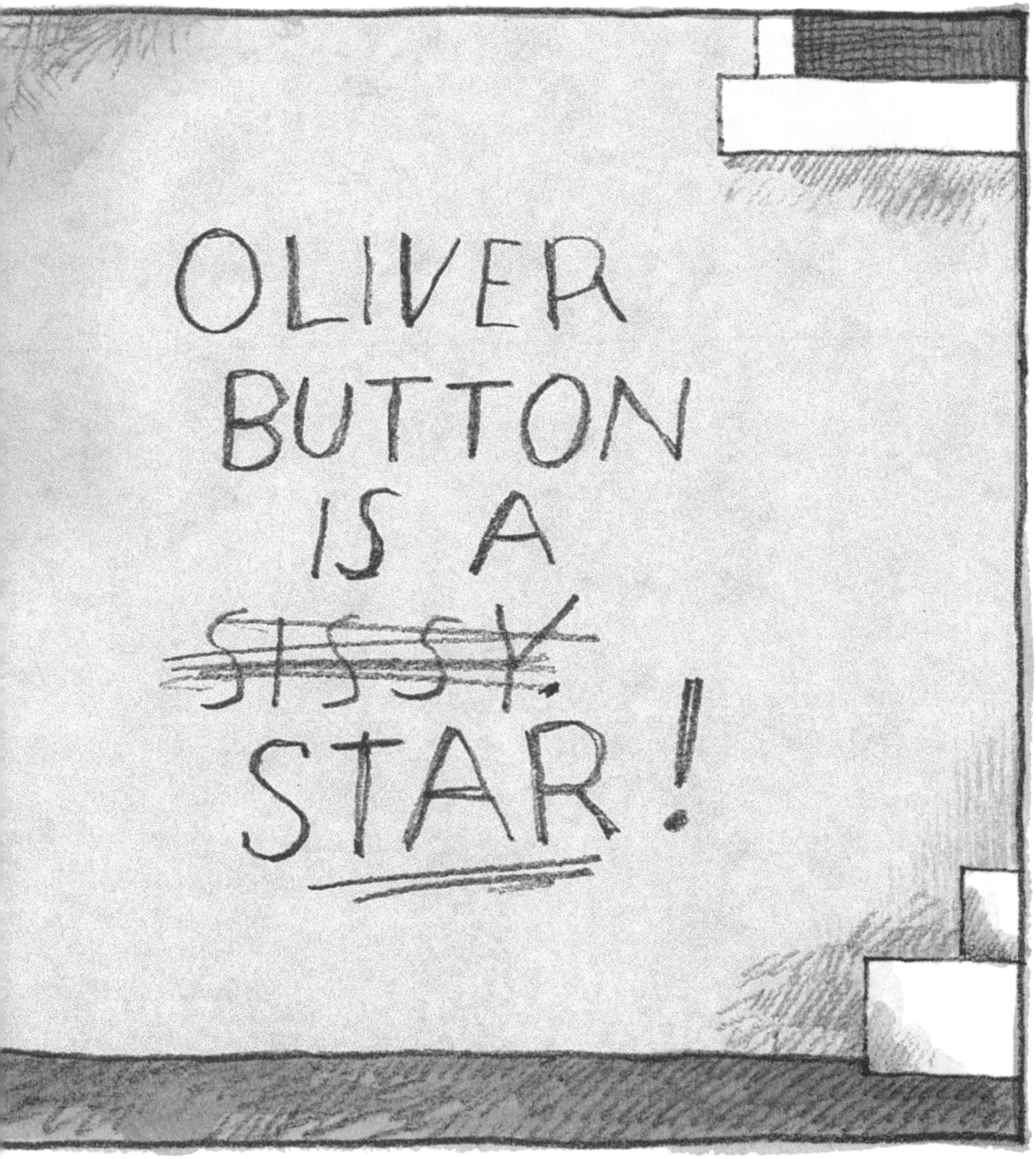
OLIVER
BUTTON
IS A
~~SISSY.~~
STAR!